To

From

Written and illustrated by Kate Toms.
Designed by Annie Simpson and Karen Morrison.

Incy Wincy spider

Kate Toms

make
believe
ideas

Incy Wincy
Spider

went UP the water spout.

DOWN came the rain,
and washed the spider OUT.

Out came the SUN

and dried up all the rain,

so Incy Wincy Spider

climbed up the spout again.

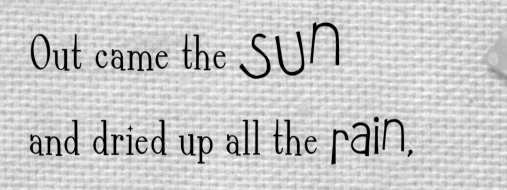

Here we go again!

But why does **INCY** climb the **spout?**

(In case you are in any doubt.)

Because he's **SPUN** his web up **high,**

so he can **see** the **world** go by . . .

(It's easy **dropping** to the floor,
but climbing **UP** is quite a chore.)

Incy Wincy Spider

doesn't like the **rain**,

he's got his **swimming goggles** on,

(he won't get caught again).

But . . . just as he starts climbing UP the water spout, another shower of rain falls down and washes Incy out!

Uh-oh!

Now **Incy's** trying once again,

umbrella **at the ready**,

the **rain** won't beat him **this** time

if he takes it

nice and **steady**.

Looking round, what's **Incy** seen?
A round and **bouncy** trampoline!

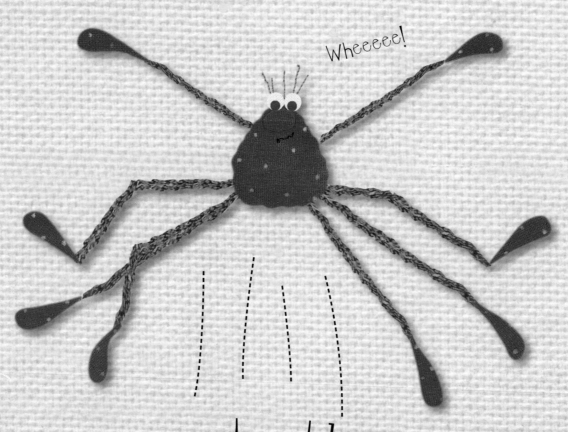

Wheeeee!

He's found a way to get home fast...

Over the hedge,
over the wall,
a stripy tent
breaks his fall.

Looking puzzled,
Incy thinks.
He rubs his hairy head and blinks.

The washing's out, the weather's fine,

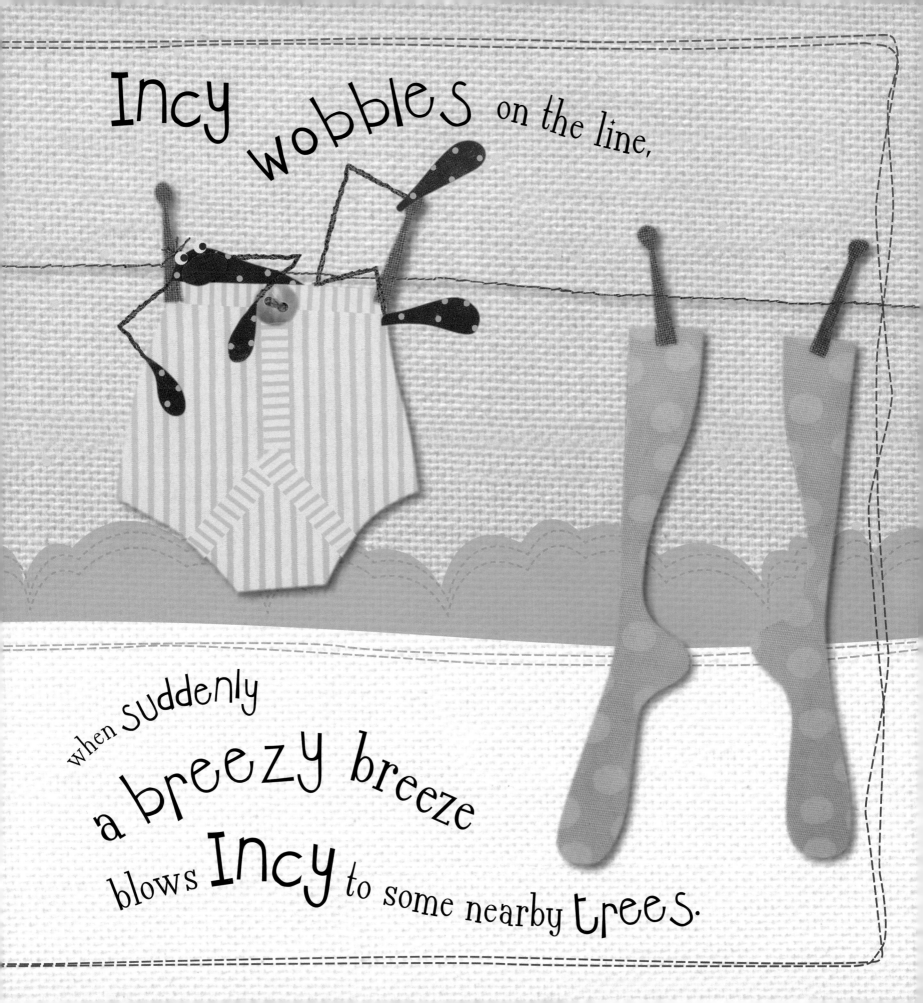

Incy wobbles on the line,

when suddenly a breezy breeze blows Incy to some nearby trees.

Through the leaves,
Incy spies
several pairs of
beady eyes.

"But **worse** than that,"
Incy squeaks,

Incy's running, quite puffed out,

but in the distance,

sees the

spout.

It's the best idea he's had all day.

He'll climb the spout another way.

The rain comes down

Back in his web,

he's **happy** now.

(It's easy when you've worked out how . . .)

The lesson learned?
Try, try again . . . .

and don't be put off by the rain!

So **Incy Wincy Spider**
can **climb** the water spout.
And even if the **rain pours down**,
it can't wash **Incy** out.

For **Incy Wincy Spider**

has found **another** way,

and now it's "easy-peasy"